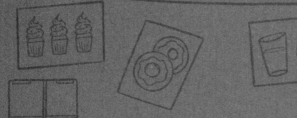

BITE THE BAGEL

ALLEY & Rex

BITE THE BAGEL

written by
JOEL ROSS

illustrated by
NICOLE MILES

Atheneum Books for Young Readers

NEW YORK LONDON TORONTO SYDNEY NEW DELHI

$\mathcal{A}$
atheneum

ATHENEUM BOOKS FOR YOUNG READERS • An imprint of Simon & Schuster
Children's Publishing Division • 1230 Avenue of the Americas, New York, New York
10020 • This book is a work of fiction. Any references to historical events, real people, or
real places are used fictitiously. Other names, characters, places, and events are products
of the author's imagination, and any resemblance to actual events or places or persons,
living or dead, is entirely coincidental. • Text © 2022 by Joel Ross • Illustration © 2022
by Nicole Miles • Cover design © 2022 by Simon & Schuster, Inc. • All rights reserved,
including the right of reproduction in whole or in part in any form. • ATHENEUM
BOOKS FOR YOUNG READERS is a registered trademark of Simon & Schuster,
Inc. Atheneum logo is a trademark of Simon & Schuster, Inc. • For information about
special discounts for bulk purchases, please contact Simon & Schuster Special Sales at
1-866-506-1949 or business@simonandschuster.com. • The Simon & Schuster Speakers
Bureau can bring authors to your live event. For more information or to book an event,
contact the Simon & Schuster Speakers Bureau at 1-866-248-3049 or visit our website
at www.simonspeakers.com. • Also available in an Atheneum Books for Young Readers
hardcover edition • The text for this book was set in Aldus. • The illustrations for
this book were rendered digitally. • Manufactured in the United States of America •
0123 MTN • First Atheneum Books for Young Readers proprietary paperback
January 2023 • 10 9 8 7 6 5 4 3 2 1 • The Library of Congress has cataloged
the hardcover edition as follows: • Names: Ross, Joel N., 1968– author. | Miles, Nicole,
illustrator. • Title: Bite the bagel / Joel Ross ; illustrated by Nicole Miles. • Description:
First edition. | New York : Atheneum Books for Young Readers, [2022] | Series: Alley &
Rex ; book 2 | Audience: Ages 8 to 12. | Summary: Prankster Alley and bunny-suited
brainiac Rex help each other survive PE and save the breakfast cart. • Identifiers: LCCN
2021053971 | ISBN 9781534495470 (hardcover) | ISBN 9781534495494 (ebook) •
Subjects: CYAC: Schools—Fiction. | Behavior—Fiction. | Individuality—Fiction. |
Friendship—Fiction. | Humorous stories. | LCGFT: Novels. | Humorous fiction. •
Classification: LCC PZ7.1.R677 Bi 2022 | DDC [Fic]—dc23 • LC record available at
https://lccn.loc.gov/2021053971 • ISBN 9781665938358 (PJ Our Way prop. edition)

To my brother Dylan,
an expert in questionable
culinary decisions!
—N. M.

I love mornings.

Specifically, I love missing them because I'm still in bed. I've got nothing against rosy dawns and chirping birds—I just enjoy them most while asleep.

Can you spot me in that picture?

Look closer.

Did you find me yet?

Here's a clue: no, you didn't, because I'm not there.

I'm already in the kitchen, staring into the fridge.

"What are you doing up so early?" my mother asks me.

"Monna mushon," I tell her.

"You're on a mission?" she says.

"Muh," I agree.

She points her toast at me. "Are you trying to write 'ALIEN PARKING' in duct tape on the school roof again?"

"Guh," I say.

My dad forks his cheese blintz. "He's going to eat Frooty Noodles cereal at the free breakfast cart until his brain explodes."

"Mah," I say, then sleepwalk to my bike.

And roughly a thousand hours before the first bell rings, I arrive at Blueberry Hill School, as bright-eyed and bushy-tailed as a chipmunk in a firecracker factory.

That's me. My name is Alley Katz, and my mission is this: elite training for my friend Rex.

I'm in sixth grade and Rex is in fourth, but we have lots in common. For example, he's skipped a few grades, and *I've* skipped a few classes. Also, he wears a bunny suit to school every day, and I have a *friend* who wears a bunny suit to school every day.

See? We're like twins!

On the other hand, my favorite class is PE. Frankly, I think every period needs more squeaking sneakers and screaming chaos. But Rex isn't a fan of the bouncing and the yelling. Not with dodgeball starting this week.

That's why I'm here, to train him in the Art of the Dodge.

I have everything I need: one brick wall, two soccer balls, a soft football, a whiffle ball, seven pairs of tightly rolled socks, a bunch of water balloons (empty), and a shampoo bottle that I forgot to put in the recycling.

Also, a few rolls of duct tape, in case I accidentally find myself on the roof. (Thanks for reminding me, Mom!)

However, the grand total of Rexes is zero.

Of him, I have none.

So I wait patiently for six or seven seconds, then head for the breakfast cart to grab some Frooty Noodles. (Thanks for reminding me, Dad!)

Every morning before school, the lunch ladies wheel a cart into the courtyard outside the cafeteria for an extra bonus snack. There's fruit, cereal, bagels, drinks, and granola bars for needy kids— and for kids whose parents buy cereal that tastes like unsweetened twigs. Everyone's welcome!

During my first few years at Blueberry Hill,

my mom dropped me off on her way to work every morning, and I'd raid the cart. My stomach still remembers and growls happily when I reach the courtyard.

Then the rest of me growls unhappily.

Because this is what I see:

1) a bunch of kids I recognize—mostly fifth, sixth, and seventh graders

2) a bunch of younger kids I don't recognize—a knee-high forest of piping voices and two-ton backpacks

3) posters for a school fundraiser

FUNDRAISER BAKE SALE THIS THURSDAY! 2-4 PM COME TO THE GYM FOR DELICIOUS TREATS

SIGN UP IN THE OFFICE BY TUESDAY

(Here's some BONUS EDUCATIONAL CON-TENT! You see that word "fundraiser"? I just learned that's *fund*-raiser, not *fun*-draiser. Why? Why do grown-ups always take the *fun* out of everything?)

4) locked cafeteria doors
5) the big TV screen in the cafeteria window scrolling School News of the Day
6–32) candy wrappers and trees and walkways and loads of other stuff

Yet there's one thing I don't see. I mean, I look *directly* at where it isn't and still can't find it.
The breakfast cart is gone.

2

I stagger closer and say, "What? How? Where?"

"Alley Katzenjammer!" Mouse bellows, which answers exactly zero of my questions. "No bagels!"

"I see that," I say. "But *why*?"

"Because the cart isn't here," Mouse bellows. "It's still in the cafeteria."

"Aha!" I say, spotting the problem immediately. "But the cafeteria is locked."

"With the cart inside," Mouse bellows, raising her tennis racket over her head.

Mouse plays every sport in school—the whole A to Z, from basketball to badminton. She's small and bouncy, like a Super Ball with a ponytail, and even though she's in sixth grade, she's stronger than most eighth graders.

Also, her volume is stuck at ten. When she calls for a time-out, kids in the next state take a break.

"C'mere, I'll show you!" she bellows, and whacks an imaginary tennis ball toward me.

I "return" her pretend serve, and we volley over to the cafeteria window. Then I press my face against the glass and spot a familiar shape.

"The lunch ladies forgot to wheel out the cart." I shove her imaginary tennis ball into my pocket, in case I need it later. "They're going to feel pretty bad when they realize."

"I feel pretty bad now," Mouse bellows. "I need the cart for second breakfast."

"For some kids it's *first* breakfast," I tell her.

A wave of hungry little kids swirls around our ankles like a gap-toothed tide. They peer through the window, and their squeaky voices say things like, "There's food on the cart! Cereal! Juice boxes!"

"Bagels!" Mouse bellows. "If only we could get inside . . ."

That's when a plan springs fully formed into my brain.

I don't want to brag, but I'm pretty good at planning. In fact, I once heard Principal Kugelmeyer say, "Alley thinks 'planning ahead' means 'checking if you have a parachute *after* you jump from the plane.'"

Parachutes? Cool.

Free fall? Awesome!

"Give me a lift," I tell Mouse, and point upward.

Have you ever noticed those wide windows above some doors? The ones that open like see-saws? They're how teachers talked to each other before email: by messenger pigeon.

Of course, now there's a better use for them.

Anyway, I happen to know, from the four or five times that I accidentally climbed through one of those windows, that I can climb through one of those windows.

All I need is a desk or chair . . . or a kid as strong as Mouse.

She weaves her fingers together. I step onto her hands, balancing myself on her shoulder, and she hefts me toward the window.

I'm almost there when an urgent voice across the courtyard says, "Alllley!"

3

Urgent voices usually say "Alllley!" in one of three ways.

The first is a whisper: *Alllley, drop the frogs— the teacher's coming!*

The second is a chant: *Al-ley, Al-ley, Al-ley,* like while I'm trying to break the school's Toilet Paper Unraveling record.

The third is a roar like Poseidon while he prongs a foolish mortal with his trident. I get that one from . . . pretty much all adults.

This particular "Alllley!" sounds extremely tridential . . . but it's a kid's voice.

So I squirm around Mouse and see my friend Chowder glaring at me from across the courtyard.

"What do you think you're doing?" he barks.

I don't know if you've met Chowder, but he rarely glares or barks. He is a gentle soul, more into gazing and cooing, so this takes me by surprise.

"What does it look like?" I ask him.

"I'll tell you what it looks like!" he snaps.

"Okay, what?"

"I'll tell you!"

"So tell me!"

"I will!" he says, then flushes Valentine's Day pink and says, "It looks like you—you're up to no good!"

I don't know if you caught that, but my eagle eye spotted a clue. *Valentine's Day* pink?

He's in love again! I don't know who he's crushing on this time. Maybe one of the seventh-grade boys, maybe one of the sixth-grade girls. Though probably not Mouse, because he once recited a love poem to her in science class, and they say that, even now, if you put a beaker to your ear you can hear her laughing.

"I'm not up to no good," I assure him.

"Ha!" he says.

"I'm up to good."

"Ha *ha!*" he says. "Like I don't believe my own eyes! You—you're . . ."

"I'm breaking into the cafeteria. The lunch ladies forgot to bring out the cart."

He blinks at me. "Really?"

"Yeah."

"Oh, cool," he says. "Grab me a juice box."

Then he smiles in my general direction, the extra-drippy smile that he saves for his crushes. I'm not sure who he's aiming at, but it looks like he's two seconds from cooing, so I don't wait around.

I tell Mouse to lift me higher, then I squirm through the window. I drop to the cafeteria floor and land like a cat: on all fours, with my butt in the air.

Then I creep to the breakfast cart and distribute the goodies in an orderly fashion.

There's only one snag.

Mouse makes a gentle suggestion: "THROW ANOTHER BOX OF CEREAL, ALLEY! THAT ONE EXPLODED!"

She's so loud that the building shakes.

She's so loud that jackhammers cover their ears.

She's so loud that her voice punches a hole through the multiverse into a different dimension. Frankly, I'm lucky that the tentacled sheep of Earth 9 don't start trotting through.

EARTH 4   EARTH VII

Less luckily: a yard monitor *does* start trotting through. He marches into the courtyard and gapes at the fog of vaporized Wheatie-Os from the cereal box that burst.

So what I do is, I panic.

Instead of hiding in the cafeteria, I hurl myself at the window.

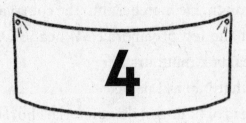

4

I slam against the glass like a sixth-grade bug on a truck windshield.

I pull myself upward, squeeze halfway through the pizza window—and freeze.

The yard monitor is too close! If I drop into the courtyard, he'll see me for sure. But if I stay here, he'll also see me, also for sure.

Now, I know what you're thinking.

You're thinking, *Tentacled sheep? So cool!*

And to you I say, "They're not only cool—they're also warm. After all, they're the source of tentacled *wool*."

But what you're forgetting is that I'm currently trapped in a window. Please try to keep up.

If I move in either direction, I'll get caught. Yard monitors are attracted to motion.

I'm doomed!

And then I see it: salvation.

In other words: a banana stuck on the window beside me.

If cartoons have taught me one thing, it's that no force on earth can resist the slipperiness of a banana peel. Others might pause to think. Not me. Thinking is exactly what I don't pause to do.

I unwrap that banana faster than a seven-armed monkey (also from Earth 9) and huck the peel to the ground at the yard monitor's feet.

And you know what happens next?

The yard monitor says, "Hey! Did one of you break into the cafeteria?"

There is the sound of twenty-two kids absolutely not looking in my direction.

The yard monitor scowls at Mouse. He scowls at Chowder—who is, for some reason, doing jumping jacks. He scowls at the posters for the bake sale, at the walkways and the TV screen and the rest.

Then he steps on the banana peel.

For a moment, my world is perfect. The bottom of his shoe touches the top of the peel, and the heavens play air guitar.

But then . . . he doesn't slip.

Let me repeat that while you reattach your head: he doesn't slip. He doesn't even notice. He just squashes the peel and *takes another step.*

I stare in horror at the ruins of my childhood. The cloud of cereal dust turns into a white mist of dread. The abyss raises its scaly head to stare at me—

And by "abyss," I mean the yard monitor.

He's three milliseconds from noticing me, so I do the only thing that makes sense. I try to look like I'm *supposed* to be dangling with my head in the courtyard and my butt in the cafeteria.

And then a voice says, "I beg your pardon, but I am concerned about the deleterious effects of airborne wheat particles on students with allergies."

And there, across the courtyard, a floppy-eared angel appears.

5

Rex's eyes shine with the uncanny brilliance of a kid who eats carrots on purpose. His briefcase gleams, his whiskers twitch, and I know that I am saved.

I don't know *why*, though. I mean, half the words he just said are gibberish.

Still, the yard monitor gasps, "Allergies!"

Oh, *that's* why. Teachers panic when you mention the word "allergies." Heck, they won't let you in the front doors if you're even *dressed* as a peanut. (Though for the record, I was dressed as an earthworm.)

The yard monitor plunges into the Wheatie-O cloud and yells at the kids to stay back, like some kind of hero.

And I, like a completely different kind of hero, tumble into the courtyard . . . and am plucked from the air by Mouse, who plants me sneaker-side down.

"Thanks," I say.

"Thanks so much," Chowder tells her. "So, so much. Good catch, ha ha!"

"Due to cutbacks," the yard monitor announces, "the supplementary nutritional service is ending."

"Due to what the what what are what?" Mouse bellows, neatly summarizing my own question.

"The breakfast cart is closing," the yard monitor says. "Yesterday was the last day."

A tragic murmur ripples through the crowd of little kids.

"No bagels?" Mouse bellows.

I hear dozens of tiny hearts break. I am drowning in a sea of big, sad eyes. (Not literally. That would be gross. Eyeballs everywhere.)

Then the yard monitor says, "Who climbed into the cafeteria? Where's Alley? Is Alley here?"

By the time he hits that third question mark, the answer is no. I'm not there. I'm somewhere else. Being somewhere else is one of my gifts. Seriously, if you ever need someone to not be somewhere, just text me and I won't come.

Where I am, instead of there, is at the brick wall again.

But this time, there is a positive number of Rexes. I mean one. A single Rex. He's there—that's all I'm saying.

"Up against the wall," I tell him, tossing a cheerful rolled-up sock in his direction. "Let's get training."

Rex deflects the sock with his briefcase. "I believe you're laboring under a misapprehension."

"You bet!" I tell him, and unpillowcase a soccer ball.

"My trepidation regarding PE class," Rex says,

"is not related to my ability to elude projectiles."

"You can say that again," I tell him.

He does—and his vocabulary hits me like a dictionary between the eyes.

"Well, then!" I say, when the dizziness stops. "Are you ready? I brought everything we need."

He blinks at me. "You woke early for the sole purpose of teaching me to dodge balls?"

"I expect great things from you," I tell him. "You were born to hop. Are you ready?"

"Indeed," he says, and I launch my attack.

I attack gently, though, because I don't want to scare him. Imagine a sleepy kitten lobbing cotton candy around: that's how hard I launch.

Rex bobs and weaves. He is a blur of bunny suit and briefcase.

"I see you follow the Way of the Rabbit," I tell him, and turn the Launch Knob to three.

He still dodges every throw, so I add a whiffle ball to the mix, and a little conversation.

"Those little kids need breakfast," I say as Rex bounds away from an underhanded shampoo bottle. "You can't learn when you need to nosh."

"If you need to what?" Rex asks.

"Nosh," I explain. "Eat. I mean, they can't focus if they're hungry."

"I believe that the adverse effects of hunger on education," he says, ducking a sudden football, "are well established in the literature."

That almost stops me, but I recover by chucking Mouse's imaginary tennis ball at him and following up with a rapid fire of socks.

He dodges with ease, his ears quivering. "You have yet to connect!"

He's loving this! So I crack my knuckles and say, "You've just been lucky so far!"

"So have you," Chowder tells me, trotting around the corner.

"What?" I say.

"Huh?" he says.

"Well—what?"

"Um," he says. "Huh?"

I cast my mind into the mists of history, trying to remember how this conversation started. Then I repeat the first thing he heard: "You've just been lucky so far?"

"So have you!" Chowder tells me. "So, so lucky. I saw you falling from that cafeteria window. Saved at the last moment by a—" He gulps like a lovestruck bullfrog. "A goddess."

"I have no idea what you're talking about," I say. "But *we're* talking about the breakfast cart."

"There are no bagels!" Chowder says, outraged. "What if someone wants a second breakfast?"

"What if someone wants a first one?" I say.

"It is indeed unfortunate," Rex says.

I frown. It's worse than unfortunate. It's unfair and ungood. Blueberry Hill School is better than this.

"No way," I say.

"No way what?" Chowder says.

"No way are they closing down that cart!"

6

Rex coughs. "How do you propose to reverse the decision?"

"You mean, how am I going to save the cart?" I ask.

"That's a good question," Chowder says.

"And here's a good answer!" I tell him, but I have no idea what to say next.

Chowder peers at me curiously. Rex peers at me curiously. Heck, *I'd* peer at me curiously, except I never give in to peer pressure.

"We'll start bringing in our own food," I hear myself say after a long and thoughtful pause. "At least until we get the cart back. Oranges and granola bars and—"

"Bagels!" Chowder says.

I look from him to Rex, except Rex isn't there. He must've rabbitted off during my long and thoughtful pause.

"Well, I don't know about that . . . ," I say.

"Bagels," Chowder repeats.

"They're not as easy as fruit or—"

"Bagels are the fruit of *love*," he says. "That's why they're shaped like hearts."

"They're not shaped like hearts."

"Bagels," he says. "Bagels, bagels, bagels!"

"Fine!" I say.

"BEEEEEP," the second bell says, which means we're late for class.

It also means the first bell must've rung during that long and thoughtful pause, but I can't keep track of everything around here.

The school day happens. There are desks and classes and teachers—and probably even lessons.

I'm 82 percent sure that Mr. Kapowski, my English teacher, asks us to discuss the reading with our partner. I think that's why I'm sitting with Maya, and other kids are schmoozing instead of listening to a lesson.

I can't remember exactly, because I'm distracted by the Bagel Question.

"Which is," I explain to Maya, "'How do I bring dozens of bagels to school without any money?'"

"Every single day," she says, not looking up from the phone hidden in her book.

Phones aren't allowed at school, but Maya doesn't care. She's playing her game—*Realm Ruler*—even though if she's caught one more time, her parents will take her phone away.

She right about the "every single day" thing, though.

"That's like a hundred bagels a week," I say.

"Craft your own bagels," she tells me. "Like I craft squid-skin potions in my *Realm Ruler* queendom."

"I don't know how," I say.

She swipes at her phone. "You take three green-flower herbs and—"

"I mean I don't know how to craft bagels!" I say. "Not squid-skin potions."

"What do you want *bagels* for?" she asks, still not looking up.

"Oh forget it," I mutter, but I don't forget it. I think about it. "Can *you* craft bagels?"

"I don't know," Maya says. "I've never tried. I'll ask around."

"Ask who?"

She taps at her screen. "You know the new tavern in my game?"

"The *Realm Ruler* chat room," I say, because she's told me about this updated feature nineteen thousand times.

"It's more than a chat room! There are meetings and contests and . . . oh." She peers at her screen. "You can't craft bagels in-game."

"I'm talking about the real world, Maya."

She doesn't hear me. "But if you find a similar foodstuff, you can change it around."

"What does that even mean, 'a similar foodstuff'?"

"Start with something that's *like* a bagel, then

make it bagelier. Like upgrading a bucket into a helmet or a shoe into a boot."

"Those aren't foodstuffs," I grumble, but I start wondering what might work.

Wait a second.

Back up. Look at that last one. A *doughnut* is bagel shaped. That's a totally similar foodstuff!

And Bubbie, my sweet and helpful grand-mother, lives in the Land of Free Doughnuts. You can't throw a denture in her senior center with-out hitting a doughnut.

I know. I've tried.

Doughnuts aren't allowed at school, because they're too tasty, but that's okay. I'm not plan-ning to bring *doughnuts* to school.

"Doughnuts," I murmur, feeling the sprinkles of a brilliant idea.

"Alley and Maya," Mr. Kapow says, "why don't you share with the class?"

7

I'm a big fan of sharing. If you see me with a box of cookies or an armload of water balloons, you don't even need to ask.

What's mine is yours.

But that's not what Mr. Kapow means. He wants us to stand in front of the class and talk about our reading. That's not sharing—sharing is giving *other people* a chance to talk!

I explain this to Mr. Kapow, but he misses the point. Honestly, sometimes I wonder about teachers.

"Your reading?" he says.

I look at Maya.

Maya looks at I.

We've been friends since the second grade, so

I know that Maya's smart but lazy. ("The exact opposite of Alley," I once heard a teacher say. Meaning that I'm lazy but smart.) She hasn't done the reading either. Even worse, as we stand from our table, she slips her phone into her book to take with her.

I give her a look like, *Leave that here!*

She gives me a look like, *I can't!*

I give her a look like, *Why not?*

She gives me a look like, *For reasons I can't explain in a look!*

Then we slouch together to the front of the class.

I clear my throat and rattle off an introduction: "Well! Well, well, well."

Now that we're officially introduced, I'm going to let Maya have a turn. Except she opens her book an inch to peek at her phone—while we're standing in front of the teacher!

"Maya!" I whisper without moving my lips.

"I'm busy!" she whispers back. "There's a big meeting at the Goblin's Hug."

At least, I *think* that's what she says.

The Sobbing Slug? The Cobbler's Shrug?

It's hard to tell, because: A) she's not in a big meeting—she's in the middle of English class, and B) SHE'S NOT IN A BIG MEETING—SHE'S IN THE MIDDLE OF ENGLISH CLASS!

And so am I. So I keep talking to the other kids: "I'll start by sharing the—the subject. Of the reading."

"We're talking about family today," Mr. Kapow says.

"Exactly!" I tell him. "Well done!"

"Alllley," he says, and with a certain urgent tone in his voice. "Share one example from the reading."

"Coming right up," I say, then can't remember any words in English.

"Did the reading surprise you at all?" Mr. Kapow prompts me.

"You bet," I say. "Especially the parts about families. Parents, siblings. Cousins!"

He sighs. "Forget the example. Just tell us what you're thinking, Alley. How about that?"

I like Mr. Kapow, so I try really hard. What

am I thinking? For a moment, I draw a blank. Heck, I don't stop at drawing it. I make a complete 3D model of the blank, then add shading and animation.

I CAPTURED ITS ESSENTIAL BLANKNESS

Then, out of nowhere, I realize exactly what I'm thinking!

And I say, "What *are* bagels?"

Nobody answers. Even Mr. Kapow just gapes at me.

"The salty cousin of the doughnut!" I announce.

And that's when Maya's phone slips from her book and plummets toward to the floor.

8

Have you ever heard the saying "Time marches on"?

I'm here to tell you that sometimes Time stops for a snack. Sometimes Time plops onto the couch and watches TV. Right now, Time takes a brief nap, with the phone hanging in midair and Maya frozen in horror.

What she knows, and what I know . . . in short, what we *both* know is that in the awed silence after my bagel/doughnut/cousin speech, the clatter of a phone hitting the floor will sound like two frying pans in a clothes dryer.

(MORE BONUS EDUCATIONAL CONTENT: Do not dry frying pans in a clothes dryer! For highly technical reasons, this will not work.)

To cover the noise, I howl, "DoooOOoo-OOOOooooughNUT coouUUuuSINS!"

I don't know if you'll ever need to yodel "doughnut cousins" in class. If so, here's some advice: do not gesture along wildly. And if you do gesture along wildly, *really* don't backhand a globe off a nearby table with all your might.

On the bright side, it's a nice, clean hit.

The globe takes flight. Nobody notices Maya's phone, not with the entire world, from north pole to south, hurtling above rows of students then ricocheting off a bookshelf toward the window.

It's three inches from shattering the glass when Mouse bellows, "GRAND SLAM, ALLEY!" and tackles it to the floor.

The good news is Maya grabs her phone before Mr. Kapow sees it.

The even *better* news is, after Mr. Kapow sends me to the principal's office, an awesome new plan bursts into my mind like a sneeze in a sleeping bag.

I call it plan A, for Ask.

I don't need to craft my own bagels. I just need to Ask the principal to save the breakfast cart.

• • • •

Approximately 97.1 percent of the kids at Blueberry Hill School don't know Principal Kugelmeyer. At least not as well as I do. We talk all the time, and have since the Gummy Worms versus Pencil Sharpeners incident in first grade.

"I'm just saying," I tell her, after sitting across her desk, "that sending kids to you as a punishment is rude. Like you're a monster."

"Most students," she says, looking a little tired, "don't enjoy my company as much as you do."

"Don't feel bad. They just don't know you well enough."

She looks tireder. "Alley . . ."

"Right here!" I report.

"Could you just . . . *not*? For two weeks?"

I don't know what she means, but I say, "You bet."

"I'm wrestling with a new budget, and I don't need another headache."

"Is that why you look so tired?" I ask.

She looks tiredest. "Yes, Alley."

"Do you want me to take a whack at it?"

"At what?"

"Wrestling the butt-thingy."

"The *budget*, Alley. The school's finances. How much money we have."

"Oh," I say, and a terrible thought occurs to me. "Wait a second . . ."

She eyes me. "Yes?"

"Is that why you shut down the breakfast cart? For *money*?"

She sighs and says a bunch of words.

"So, let me get this straight," I say, once she winds down. "You're closing the free breakfast cart?"

"Yes," she says.

I can't believe my ears. "As in, the cart of free breakfast?"

"Yes," she says.

"So you admit it!"

"We can't afford the supplementary nutrition program right now," she says.

"I think I speak for all the cart kids," I tell her, "when I say, *'Dude!'*"

"There's also not enough money," she says, "to replace a window if a certain student breaks it while climbing into the cafeteria before school."

9

"Oh," I say.

"At the risk of cutting himself badly," the principal says.

I squirm a little. "So that's the kind thing to 'not'?"

"Exactly," she says. "*Very* don't."

I duck my head and look at her desk. There's not much there but a sheet of blank paper with her name on it. Nothing could be boring-er, yet I keep looking at it. And I actually learn something: her first initial is *O.*

O. Kugelmeyer. Which is OK for short, but this probably isn't the best time to point that out.

"Sorry," I finally say.

She sighs again. "You've got a big heart, Alley...."

Then she pauses. Which is weird because I once heard her say, "Alley's got a big heart and also, one presumes, a brain."

This time she says, "I can't remember why you're here."

"To get in trouble for throwing a globe in Mr. Kapow's class."

"That doesn't sound like you."

"There were extending circumstances," I say, which is a phrase Rex taught me. It means "It's not my fault."

"Extenuating," Principal Kugelmeyer says.

"Circumstances," I say, joining in.

She almost smiles. "So . . . what do you think?"

"I'd give me a week's detention," I admit.

"One day's enough," she tells me. "Because of the circumstances."

"Totally extending," I tell her.

"Go!" she says, but she looks a little less tired.

That part is good. What's bad is that she didn't save the breakfast cart. Plan A didn't work, so it's time for . . .

PLAN B

I'll bring bagels to school even if I have to craft them.

I'm thinking about that as I slip from the principal's room into the front office, which, for Important Reasons, I will now describe in boring detail:

There's a floor and a ceiling. There are a few doors, one to the principal's office. There's a bench that I think of as *my* bench. There's a counter that mostly separates the office from the foyer. There are a few plants, an overworked coffee maker, and a couple of secretaries, Ms. D and Mr. D. (Not related even though they're both Ds.)

There are cubbies where the teachers get mail.

There's also the phone that I use to call Bubbie to pick me up after detention. My parents complain that I'm disorganized, but I've got this down to a precise science.

Do something interesting.

Get detention.

Call Bubbie to pick me up after detention.

Grab an ice cream on the way home.

My favorite precise sciences always end with ice cream.

Bubbie's pickup screeches to a halt in the school driveway. Well, and also on the sidewalk. She drives the way toddlers color: mostly inside the lines.

"What meshugas did you get into this time?" she asks when I climb into the passenger seat.

Meshugas mean "silliness," so I start by saying,

"The school isn't doing a free breakfast cart anymore."

She slams on the gas in disapproval, and we squeal away. "That's terrible! I've heard there's no such thing as a free lunch, but *breakfast*?"

"Yeah, so . . . instead of getting ice cream, can we go to your place for doughnuts?"

"You want doughnuts?"

"I *need* doughnuts."

"How about halvah?" she asks.

Halvah, in case you don't know, is a sesame-based dessert that tastes like sweetened sand. But also kind of good. But still like sweetened sand.

"That's not a similar foodstuff!" I tell her. "I need doughnuts. Dozens of them."

I guess I don't explain absolutely everything about plan B to Bubbie. Like, that I'm going to craft bagels to bring to school. Other people might ask questions, but Bubbie just shifts into warp 17. We don't exit hyperspace until we reach her apartment.

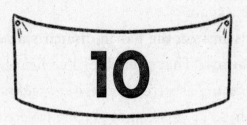

10

Bubbie and Zayde—my grandfather—live in a seniors-only place that's more like a summer camp than an apartment building. Kids aren't allowed, so I pull one of Zayde's flat caps low over my face.

When my disguise is complete, I look exactly like a kid wearing his grandfather's cap. Nobody says anything, though. Well, people say things, but not about me being a kid.

For example, they say:

Bubbie: "We need doughnuts!"

Mr. Morris: "So we'll deal you in."

Zayde: "Look at me, Alley—I'm sewing!"

Mr. Morris: "You need doughnuts?"

Me: "And garlic salt."

Mr. Morris: "That's the best kind of salt. Now pull up a chair."

Hm. That doesn't make much sense if you don't also know what I'm seeing.

Zayde is at one of the new sewing machines, making what looks like an ear warmer for a hippo, while Mr. Morris is playing poker with Mrs. Green and some other seniors.

That doesn't surprise me. Old people *love* gambling. What surprises me is the heap of doughnuts in front of them. They're using them as poker chips.

Mr. Morris gives me and Bubbie five doughnuts each, and we play for a while.

Bubbie starts winning—and teasing Zayde when his sewing goes wrong.

"I used to work as a dress cutter," Mr. Morris tells us. "In the forties."

"The *nineteen* forties?" I ask. "What are you, a hundred?"

"Closing in," he tells me.

"What's a dress cutter?" I ask.

"The person who cuts fabric for clothes. The problem was, you couldn't get a job without experience."

I take a thoughtful bite of my poker chip. "Why was that a problem?"

"Because you also couldn't get experience without a job."

Huh. That's like saying you can't have dessert until you finish dinner, but also you can't have dinner until you finish dessert.

"That *is* a problem," I say. "What did you do?"

Mr. Morris looks up from his cards. "I told them I had experience. Then I got fired nine times before I learned enough to keep a job."

"Let that be a lesson to you," Bubbie tells me.

"Lie until they hire you?" I ask.

Bubbie snorts. "No! Keep trying until you succeed."

By the time we finish the game, Bubbie has twenty doughnuts, and I have a stomachache. She starts playing bridge, so I drag the loot to her kitchen and prepare plan B: crafting bagels from doughnuts.

I line my test subjects up on the Formica counter then ransack the spice cabinet like a mad scientist.

Lightning flashes; thunder crashes. Bats swarm from the tower . . . and I begin.

I pour an inch of bagel flavorings on a plate: garlic salt, poppy seeds, onion flakes, black pepper. Also, something called celery salt, which, if my calculations are correct, is a mixture of celery and salt.

The spice doesn't stick at first, so I microwave the doughnuts to soften the sugary glaze and try again.

This time the spice sticks like honey to hair. Pretty soon I have a bunch of half-melted doughnuts with thick crusts of salts and seeds.

I take a bite.

11

When my mom picks me up, I'm still crushed by the knowledge that plan B turned into plan BO. That bagel tasted like the sweatiest T-shirt in the locker room.

"What's wrong?" Mom asks.

"Plans A and B both failed," I grumble.

"If your plans are like your grades," she says, "you can count on the C."

She's mostly teasing, so I make a face at her. She has a point, though. I'm only two letters in! Does a dictionary stop after *B*? Does an alphabet?

No, and neither do I.

Plus, I know exactly what comes after *A* and *B*. Well, we *all* know what comes after *A* and *B*! I mean, it's completely obvious.

What comes next are . . . *S* and *R*.

Plan S stands for Snacks. The cart kids still need breakfast, so I'll raid my kitchen for snacks until I think of a super-genius way to save the cart.

Plan R is Rex. I'll ask him to think of a super-genius way to save the cart. That kid is 72 percent brains. (Also, 15 percent ears, 11 percent fur, 7 percent briefcase, and 34 percent magic.)

I head to school early again the next day, to bring the S and talk to the R. Well, and to continue the elite training. Rex is already a great dodger, so today I'll teach him throwing.

When I sleepwalk into the courtyard, there are almost as many kids as yesterday, milling around like sad ants on an empty picnic basket.

"Alley Katzoo!" Mouse bellows. "You didn't get expelled!"

"Why are you here?" I ask, trotting over to her and Chowder, who is doing a weird slow-motion dance. "You know there's no breakfast cart."

"Habit!" Mouse bellows. "My dads dropped me off early anyway."

"For bagels," Chowder sighs, dancing weirdly.

The milling ants murmur, "Bagels, bagels. Cereal, juice. Oranges, granola . . ."

So I pull out my Snack Pack. After all, breakfast is the most important meal of the morning.

Well, obviously I couldn't unleash my garlicky doughnuts on innocent children—or even guilty adults. On Earth 9, I'd start a franchise, but anywhere on Earths 1 through 8, a single bite is two bites too many. I can still taste the celery.

Instead, I brought PB&J sandwiches. Except PB isn't allowed at school—allergies, again—and I'm not sure about bread.

So I *really* brought pure J: jars of jam and jelly. Also, a half gallon of orange juice and all the forks in the house, because I'm not an animal.

Plan S is a success.

I celebrate by telling Chowder that he dances like a deflating beach ball.

"I'm not dancing," he says.

"Exactly," I tell him.

He stops wriggling. "I'm stretching."

"For what?" I ask.

"Not like that! Stretching my *muscles*."

"What muscles?"

He glances pinkly at Mouse, who is scrubbing jelly off a first grader's face. "You know me—I love sports! The nets, the goals, the . . . other nets!"

"Oh!" I say. "You're crushing on Mouse again?"

And instead of denying it like a normal person, he says, "The last time was just puppy love. She's not a mouse; she's a lioness."

"Who's a lioness?" Mouse bellows.

And because I'm a good friend to Chowder, I say, "A female lion."

"You," he tells her, like an absolute dorkfish.

"And you're stalking the savannah of my heart."

That's what he says, with his own personal mouth. Those actual words. I strongly suggest that you never read that sentence again.

I'm still shuddering when Rex appears at my elbow and murmurs, "The yard monitor is approaching, and I'm afraid he may look askance at your jelly distribution."

"He can look at all the skances he wants," I say. "As long as he doesn't spot *me*."

12

In two shakes of a bunny's tail, we're back at the brick wall. I need to ask Rex to help me with the cart, but first things first. Or, in this case, second things second: I'll trigger plan R *after* dodgeball practice.

So I tell Rex that his coat is looking particularly glossy this morning, then hand him the pillowcase of balls. "This time, you throw and I'll dodge."

He twitches his whiskers. "I'm not apprehensive about dodgeball, Alley."

"Why would you be?" I ask, getting into position. "After my training, you'll be competing at the highest levels."

"That is not the—"

"*Throw*, you lazy bunny!" I holler. "Throw like the wind!"

His glasses flash—which is Rex's version of a smile—and he lobs a soccer ball at me.

Sort of. I mean, the ball leaves his paw and moves in my general direction, but it's like we're underwater. I've never seen a soccer ball move so slowly. I wait at the wall while cobwebs form and seasons pass.

The soccer ball loses hope halfway to me and falls to the ground with a defeated thud.

"Nice try!" I say. "Good effort! I like your style! Now another!"

He throws again. This time the football wobbles across the ground toward my left sneaker like a dizzy snail.

"What you might not understand," I inform him, "is that the name 'dodgeball' is a what-do-you-call-it."

"You are correct that I don't understand," he says.

"A whatchamacallit," I explain. "A thingummy! One of those names that don't mean what they sound like they mean!"

"A misnomer?" he says.

"Ha ha!" I say, even though I don't get the joke. "My point is, dodging is only half the game. Throwing is the other half. And catching is the *third* half."

"That adds up to a hundred and fifty percent," Rex says, mistaking me for a math teacher.

"Maybe it does and maybe it doesn't," I tell him. "You're great at dodging, so we'll just work on throwing and catching." I pull a bunch of balloons from my pocket. "I have special gear for that."

"Balloons?" Rex asks.

"*Water* balloons, from my special collection. Once you can catch these, my cottontailed apprentice, you'll have mastered the—"

The whiffle ball bounces off my forehead, and Rex says, "Alley!"

"Good throw!" I say, rubbing my whiffled forehead.

"Alley," he repeats. "I am not concerned about dodgeball, but about the PE dress code."

"Wait. You mean you're not worried about dodgeball?"

"No."

"Dodgeball isn't what you're worried about."

"Correct."

I'm beginning to understand. "You're worried about the dress code?"

"Indeed." His ears droop unhappily. "I am obliged, by the end of this week, to don the official gym uniform or face punishment."

I'm not sure who Don is, or how he's involved, but this isn't the time to ask. Alley looks sad, which makes me mad.

"You mean you need to wear regular gym clothes by this Friday?" I ask.

"That is the precise day to which I refer."

"But you don't *want* to wear regular gym clothes."

"And that," he says, "is a truth of which I am keenly aware."

"I'll talk to them," I tell him. "The gym

teachers—the principal—Don! I don't know who this guy thinks he is, but you just point me at him."

Rex looks happy and sad at the same time. "I appreciate the offer, Alley. However, I suspect that your intervention would not resolve the issue."

"You think I won't change anyone's mind?"

"That is precisely my thinking."

"Oh. Then I'll duct-tape the gym doors shut."

Rex eyes me for a rabbity moment. "That, too, strikes me as being an exercise in futility."

That sentence goes over my head, but I make a wild grab for it, and I suspect he means that duct tape won't work.

"Hm . . ." I kick the shampoo bottle against the wall. "How about the old fill-the-bathroom-with-cabbages trick?"

Rex blinks at me. "In what manner might that improve my situation?"

"Well, it won't help with the dress code *directly*."

"And indirectly?"

"Not that either. Still! Just say the word and I'll unleash the vegetables."

"While I am moved by the offer," he says, "I must decline."

I pat his shoulder. "Don't worry. I'll think of something."

"I would prefer that you focus on reinstating the breakfast cart."

"You want me to help get the cart back?"

"Indeed."

"Huh. People usually ask me to stop helping." This is the perfect time to launch plan R, so I start by saying, "But how? All I know right now is, I'm going to need more jelly."

"I am considering a different approach," Rex says.

"What, chocolate syrup?"

"Of course not chocolate syrup."

"Have you lost your final marble?" I demand. "You want me to bring *BBQ sauce*?"

"Why on earth would I—" He takes a breath. "Am I correct in recalling that your grandmother was employed as cafeteria staff?"

"You mean, was my grandmother a lunch lady?" I ask.

"That is, indeed, the vernacular terminology."

Sometimes you need to ignore Rex's words completely. "And by grandmother you mean Grannie Blatt?"

"I do."

"Never heard of her," I say.

"She might suggest a method by which to ensure the return of the breakfast cart. That is, she might tell you how to save the cart."

"I guess," I mutter, pretty bummed that plan R is turning into plan GB. "But then I'd have to talk to her."

He gazes toward the courtyard. "I expect the younger students will soon forget the cart entirely. After attending classes, weak from hunger, without even the comfort of friendships forged in the courtyard over a granola bar or banana—"

"Okay, okay!" I say. "I'll talk to her."

His ears perk up. "I thought you might."

"Though I'd rather fill a bathroom with

cabbages," I mutter, before a happier thought occurs to me. "Hey, we've still got a few minutes before first bell!"

Rex twitches his whiskers. "That is correct."

"Are you thinking what I'm thinking?" I ask.

"I strongly suspect," he says, "that I am."

13

There is science; there is PE. There is math and lunch and English.

I probably learn loads. For example . . . well, I can't think of any examples.

Oh! Oh, except this lesson, from math class:

$$2+2=$$

I spend most of the day thinking about Grannie Blatt. I mean, Rex is right. Plan GB makes sense: she knows about school meals. She might even help.

But at what price?

She might ask me to scrub her dentures.

She might ask me to sniff her yogurt.

There is no depth to which a Blatt will not sink.

Still, I can't let my fellow breakfast-carters down. So I spend most of the day preparing myself for the showdown.

On the bright side, I also do huge amounts of *not* for Principal Kugelmeyer. I've never done this much not before. It turns out that when I really apply myself, I can achieve absolutely nothing.

By the end of the day, I've only done a grand total of two things other than worry about Grannie Blatt.

First, during gym class, I called a brief time-out to discuss the "mandatory" gym clothes rule. I calmly explained the problem. For example, what if a student prefers to wear, say, a giraffe outfit? What then?

However, the gym teacher refused to see reason.

Second, during science class, I took a pen apart—unscrewing the pointy bit, removing the spring and the ink tube—while Maya sat next to me and said, "Thanks."

I didn't know what she was talking about. (Leave your guess in the comments! I mean, not of *this*, obviously. This doesn't have comments. Just find comments somewhere and leave your guess. Also, like and subscribe.)

Still, I politely said, "Any time."

"For keeping Mr. Kapow from seeing my phone," she explained. "By punching that globe. And sorry I didn't help with the reading. I was in a meeting."

"I'm pretty sure you were in English class," I said.

She prodded her phone. "Didn't I tell you about the *Realm Ruler* update?"

"The tavern. Yeah."

She poked her phone. "There was a big meetup at the Goblin's Mug."

"Mug!" I said.

She patted her phone. "We share tips online, and there's contests, like the Monthly Mug, where you submit art or videos or costumes, and everyone votes on the best one."

"Do you win a mug?" I asked.

"No! A crown. I want one so much."

"Let me see," I said, and she showed me her phone.

Half the screen was text, where the players talk to one another. The other half was an old-time tavern, with green tapestries and stacks of barrels. Animated monsters and warriors and jesters milled around, stopping now and then to cast a spell or do a silly dance.

"The Mug has thousands of members," Maya told me. "People share cat pictures and recipes and—"

"If anyone has a recipe for bananas and granola bars, let me know."

"What for?" she asks.

As I finish taking the pen apart, I tell her that I'm talking to Grannie Blatt after school, to ask for advice about saving the breakfast cart.

"Why do you care so much?" she asked.

"Kids need breakfast! And I loved grabbing snacks when I was little, and I made friends, and it's just not fair."

"What you need is a charity fundraiser," she said.

"Fun-draiser," I said.

"Yeah," she said.

"SPLAT," the ink tube said.

"Alllllley!" Ms. Li said.

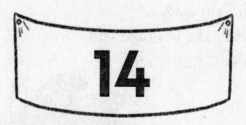

14

After school, the world blurs like someone clicked a fast-forward button; then I'm at home, talking to Grannie Blatt on FaceChat.

Me: "Your finger's covering the camera, Grannie. I can't see anything."

Her: "Alley? Nu? Are you there?"

Me: "Yes, hello! Right here!"

Her: "Where? I can't see bupkes."

Me: "On the couch? You need to press the button with the—"

Her: "Oh, I see you now."

Me: "But I can't see *you*. Your finger is covering the camera."

Her: "Don't be silly. Are you brushing your teeth? They look yellow."

Me: "I have a question."

Her: "About puberty?"

Me: "No! No, no—no. No. No."

Her: "I'll bring my book."

Me: "Please don't."

Her: "It has pictures."

Me: "It's a question about being a lunch lady!"

Her: "Well why didn't you say so?"

So I tell her about the canceled breakfast cart.

"Budget crunch," she says, and it sounds like she's scowling, but I can't tell because her thumb doesn't have eyebrows, which are the most important part of a scowl.

"Yeah," I say. "The principal has to choose between art and music and extra breakfast."

"Bah! How can you choose between feeding the mind and feeding the stomach?"

Grannie Blatt's toenails may be classed as Dread Weapons (+4 against grandsons) but she's a big believer in education.

"I know, right?" I say. "Maybe we need a charity fundraiser."

"Bah!" she says again. "*Charity.*"

I gape at her thumb. "You don't like charity?"

"Feh!" she says. "What I like is tzedakah."

"That *means* 'charity,'" I remind her.

"It means 'justice,'" she tells me. "Sometimes charity is just people showing off by giving money. They want everyone to think they're a big shot. But justice, you don't do for gratitude."

"You don't?"

"No. Justice is how things *should* be. Would you expect thanks for treating someone fairly?"

"No," I say. "But I still don't get it."

"There are five levels of tzedakah," the grand-thumb tells me. "The first is grumpily helping people if you're asked. Next is cheerfully helping, without being asked—we're getting better and better here, Alley, not worse and worse."

"I know that!"

"Just checking," she says. "Then, even better, is when the helpers don't know who is getting helped."

"Like if you give money to a *charity*," I say, "and they pass it along without anyone knowing it was you."

"Mm. Then there are the two highest forms. Can you guess what they are?"

"The ultimate and the legendary forms. Like Pokémon."

There's a pause. The thumb looks disappointed.

"The highest level of tzedakah," her voice finally says, "is where *neither* person knows who did the helping or who got helped."

"So everything's secret?"

"That's right. And nobody marches around like a big shot."

I frown at the screen. "But wait—you said there were *two* more levels."

"The last level is different," Grannie Blatt

says. "It's building such a just world that there's no *use* for charity."

"Like if everyone already has everything they need?"

"Exactly. Charity is a sign of a broken syst- *sshh-whsh-flsh!*"

Which is the sound of a toilet flushing. Grannie Blatt is calling from *inside the bathroom.*

My heart sinks; my skin crawls. My soul grabs its popcorn and races for the emergency exit.

I end the call with a trembling finger, attached to a trembling arm, which is connected to the rest of me, which is also trembling. I don't want to think about what just happened, so I don't.

Instead, I think about plan R, which turned into plan GB, which was "ask Grannie Blatt for advice about saving the breakfast cart."

Except her advice didn't help. I mean, now I know I shouldn't march around like a big shot, but that doesn't bake any bagels.

I need another plan. A quiet, sneaky one that doesn't show off.

What I need is plan H.

15

"I have a sneaky plan," I tell Rex the next morning when we meet at the flagpole in front of school. "Plan H. Also, do you want to trade snacks?"

"Let's," he says, and opens his briefcase.

He passes me a single carrot, which I take so I won't hurt his feelings, and I give him candy corn left over from Halloween.

I usually trade with Chowder, too, but last week he started bringing in popcorn.

"It's the sportiest snack," he said, which baffled me, until I realized he's crushing on Mouse.

The only problem is, he makes his own, and he's bad at popping.

"A sneaky plan to achieve which objective?" Rex asks me once the trade is complete.

"My object," I tell him, "is to save the breakfa—"

"-*ive*," he says.

"Mm?" I say.

"Object*ive*," he says.

"Overruled!" I say quick as a flash.

He tilts his head in confusion, and a few kids say "Hey" as they wander past from the drop-off spot in the driveway.

I say "Hey" back, then can't remember what we were talking about.

"You're telling me about plan H," Rex says.

"Oh, right! Well, first I need to sneak into the front office."

"Why?" he asks.

"To grab some of the principal's . . . what's that called? The stationery with her name on it? Like 'From the Desk of Principal O. Kugelmeyer, Empress of Alphabets, Lady of the Three Rs, Blueberry Hill School.'"

"I believe the word for which you are groping is 'letterhead.'"

I squint at him. "Like blockhead or egghead?"

"Not entirely," he says, and tosses a candy corn into the bunny hole. "I fail to understand your need for letterhead."

"To save the breakfast cart! That's step one. Well, I guess the real step one is waiting for the perfect moment to speed-run the office and . . ."

I trail off because that very moment turns perfect: both office secretaries walk past us, heading for—well, I don't know where. Away from the school. Every step takes them farther, or possibly further, from the office.

I clutch Rex's arm. "Keep your rabbit eyes peeled and your bunny ears perked!"

"Beg pardon?" he squeaks.

"Flash your cottontail if you see a secretary!"

Then I stroll into the school, dart to one side, and slink into the front office. Other kids might pause, awed by the grandeur: the fluorescent lights, the FUNDRAISER TOMORROW! poster, the humble dignity of the lost-and-found box.

Not I. Not me. Not Alley Katz, in any grammatical form.

I dive behind the counter, then roll and freeze. I am stealth. I am silence. I am celery scented, because there are still bagel-doughnuts in my backpack.

I strain my eardrums but hear only the gurgle of a coffeemaker. I belly-crawl toward the principal's lair and—

Well, I know she isn't here, because her car's not in the lot.

I am completely certain she's not in.

I don't worry for a second that she's crouched on her desk, tail lashing, waiting to spring.

And here's the thing.

Brace yourself.

Are you fully braced?

Then turn the page.

16

The principal is not there.

Her office is empty. I grab a few sheets of letterhead (if that's what it's really called) and rewind the speed-run.

I un-dive past the counter. I don't dart, slink, and stroll, because I'm going absolutely backward. Read this in a mirror and you'll understand:

I DART, SLINK, AND STROLL THROUGH
THE FRONT DOORS TO FREEDOM!

Rex is still standing by the flagpole, though now he's looking absolutely noncasual. If you check the Book of Opposites for "casual" you'll find a picture of a fourth grader in a bunny suit, his eyes the size of beach balls and his ears quivering with . . . wait, let me check what the opposite of "casual" is.

"Formality." That's what his ears are quivering with. They're positively quaking with the stuff.

"Good job!" I tell him. "But are you *sure* it's called letterhead?"

"I am," he says.

"You're not thinking 'lettucehead'?"

"I have never in my life, before this very moment, thought 'lettucehead.'"

"You're welcome," I say, and the bell rings.

I head to class without bothering to explain my new plan. That's okay, because H—for Heist—is so obvious. I mean, it's what anyone would do in this situation.

Plan H: forge a note from the principal that tells the lunch ladies to restart the cart, then slip it into the cafeteria mailbox in a daring heist.

• • • •

During library, I take one of the sheets of lettucehead and write:

> *Dear Lunch Ladys and Cafeteria*
> *Countesses,*
>
> *bring back the breakfast cart or*
> *SUFFER THE CONSEQUENCES!*
> *Bagels by the dozen, oranges by*
> *the truckload!*
> *Let there be Frooty Noodles!*
>
> *Yum yum,*
> *Principal Origami Kooglemire*

Well, that won't fool anyone. *I* can't forge the
note. That's okay: I'll get Rex to write one that
looks like it came from the principal.

I accidentally skip half of history class to get
Rex to write the note. Which is a problem because
the *first* time I accidentally skipped history class,
Mx. Connaty laughed when I said, "That happened in the past. It *is* history."

However, the second time, they didn't think it was nearly as funny.

And this is the third time.

Still, I eventually track Rex to the multi-purpose room, where he's sitting with his ears drooping sadly. He was told to leave gym class because he's not wearing the right clothes.

"This week is my last chance to adopt the proper attire," he says. "If I still refuse on Friday, they shall begin giving me detention."

"Detention's not so bad," I say.

"I've never gotten into trouble before," he says in a sad, whispery voice.

"I'll tell you what," I say. "Whenever you get detention, I'll get detention too. That way you won't be alone."

His eyes mist behind his glasses. "That is a generous offer, Alley, but I hesitate to—"

"Sincerely! Elephant! Washington!"

"Beg pardon?"

"You're about to say a bunch of long words at me," I explain, "but I don't care what you say. I'm still going to do it."

He says, "Oh."

"Now," I say, "back to this note."

Rex peers at what I wrote. "While I applaud your intent, I hesitate to endorse this course of action."

I can't tell if that means he *does* want to write the note or he *doesn't* want to write the note, so I say, "Great! Make it sound like an adult human wrote it. Specifically, an eighteenth-level principal with a plus-five Glare of Smiting."

His whiskers twitch. "What I mean, Alley, is that I'm afraid that this will not work."

"I'm afraid of that too, but you know what they say. *Keep trying until you succeed!*"

17

Rex tells me what a bad idea this is.

I tell him if he doesn't write the note soon, I'll miss history class completely.

So he writes:

> *Attention Cafeteria Staff:*
>
> *Good news. After a reassessment of our budgetary concerns, I am pleased to direct you to reinstate the supplementary nutrition program—i.e., the free breakfast cart—immediately.*
>
> *Sincerely,*
> *Olivia Kugelmeyer*

I'll be honest: I start skimming after "Good news." Still, if Rex says that means "Bring back the cart!" then "Bring back the cart!" is what that means.

"You are three flavors of awesome," I tell him. "Next year I'm voting for *you* for principal."

"I appreciate that, Alley. Though principals, of course, are not elected."

"This is tyranny!" I say, and when I finally burst into history class, I try to start a conversation about evil overlords.

Sadly, Mx. Connaty insists on talking about the Silk Road instead, which it turns out was not made of silk.

What the heck? I'm still reeling from the whole "Rhode Island" lie. (The state of Rhode Island—if it even *is* a state—is definitely not an island. Also, not a road.)

The next phase of plan H is tricky: I need to sneak the note into the mail cubby in the office.

So at lunch, I put together a strike team at the table in the corner. Not just a strike team, a heist force.

STRENGTH: 10   HEART: 10   TECH: 10

AIM: 10   CRINGINESS: 9   STRATEGY: 9

VOLUME: 11   SHAME: 0   FOCUS: 3

SHE'S IN IT FOR   HE'S IN IT   SHE'S IN IT BECAUSE
THE BAGELS   FOR MOUSE   SHE'S A PAL

"Where's Rex?" Chowder asks me.

"On the way," I say, even though I didn't invite Rex. He's already worried about getting in trouble for his gym clothes.

"Good," Chowder says. "We need him."

"Oh, he's not on the way *here*," I admit. "But I'm sure he's on the way somewhere."

Chowder peers at me. "So this is *your* plan?"

"From spawn point to boss fight," I say proudly.

"We're doomed," he murmurs.

"One hundred percent!" Mouse bellows.

"I thought you said Rex wrote the fake note," Maya says, looking up from her phone for once.

"He did," I say, and slap the note on the table.

There is an awed moment as they read. Chow-der murmurs, "Reassessment?"

Maya blinks repeatedly at "supplementary."

Mouse bellows, "Reinstate!"

"Okay," Maya says, with a nod. "If Rex wrote the note, we've got a chance."

"Unless Alley made the plan," Chowder grumbles.

"Think of the bagels," I tell him, and this time what I slap on the table is my plan.

18

Ten minutes later, Maya is slouching outside the office, pretending to read a book. She's in charge of strategy. She has lots of experience in *Realm Ruler*.

She eyes Ms. and Mr. D. (I really like the Ds. That's why I'd never say aloud that I think of them as Misty and Miss Dirty, which is what their names sound like if you say 'em fast.)

Maya waits for the right moment, then taps her phone.

At the *WHOOSH* sound, Mouse springs into action.

Well, she stomps around the corner, carrying a massive plant that lives across the foyer. It's taller than she is, but she's so strong that she moves pretty quickly.

She's behind the counter before Mr. D spots her.

"Isabella?" he says. "What are you—"

"I found it in the hall!" Mouse bellows. "Where it doesn't belong!"

As her voice ricochets around the foyer, she lowers the plant to the floor outside Principal Kugelmeyer's door.

Step one is complete! Now the principal can't pop out and ruin everything.

"Er," Mr. D says. "I'm not sure *that's* where it belongs either."

Maya taps her phone before either of the Ds can tell Mouse to move the plant, and this time there's a *SIGH*.

Chowder pops up from the other side of the counter. "Excuse me?"

"Yes, Charles?" Ms. D says.

Chowder gazes at Mouse and says:

Dear Isabella,
You're sweet as a marshmella.
You turn my knees to jella.
I wanna be your fella.

There's more, but I black out for a second at the sheer cringeyness.

On the bright side, both of the Ds are trapped in a syrupy web of sixth-grade romance. Paralyzed by the courtship dance of the Lesser Domestic Chowder, they can't protect the mail cubbies.

And me? I'm sitting on my bench. I've been there the whole time. The secretaries don't even notice me. They just figure I'm in trouble again.

I am camouflaged in misbehavior.

I seize the moment to dart toward the mail cubbies. But somehow—unbelievably—the effect of Chowder's poetry wears off too soon!

The secretaries start to turn toward me . . .

. . . and Maya's phone makes our emergency *CHIRP* noise.

Mouse tosses a popcorn kernel—from the bottom of Chowder's lunchbox—at the mugs beside the coffee machine. It flies across the room, between the computer and a vase of flowers.

It's a perfect shot.

The mug goes *tink*, and Ms. and Mr. D spin toward the coffeemaker. They can't help themselves.

Most kids don't know this, but I've spent months on that bench. Whenever one of the Ds makes coffee, the mugs *tink*, and the other D gazes at the coffeemaker like a starving wolf at a bowl of starving-wolf food.

Every time.

While they're looking that way, I lunge for the mailboxes.

That's when Maya makes the chirping, whooshing, and sighing noises all at once, AND she calls the school. The office phone rings; a mug *tinks*; Chowder rhymes "mouse" with "joust." I check that I'm tucking the note into the right cubby . . .

And then I do.

I tuck the note into the right cubby.

19

I'm glowing with golden victory when I meet Rex in the hall.

"My plan came together like raspberries and cream," I tell him.

"I am gratified to hear that," he says.

"You should've seen the Ds' faces when Chowder unleashed his poem. They looked like they wished they'd flunked out of secretary school."

"I shudder to imagine," he says.

"And Mouse lifted a plant the size of two redwoods—and never missed with the popcorn!"

A cloud passes over Rex's face. "She truly excels at athletics."

"Plus, Maya timed everything perfectly. She didn't even get distracted by that game tavern."

"The Goblin's Mug," he says. "I am impressed that the gaming community created such a supportive and active forum."

"Yeah. Though Maya's never won a crown at the Monthly Mugger or whatever it's called."

"No doubt she will ultimately triumph."

"You'll never guess what else is crafted of Ultimate Triumph."

His glasses flash. "I presume you are referring to yourself?"

"Wrong!" I say. "I mean *me*."

"I stand corrected."

"I didn't stand at all!" I tell him. "I leapt from my bench. I spun; I dove. I pulled the note from my pocket and shoved it into the cubby."

As I say that, I pull the note from my pocket and raise it overhead in a pose of ultimate triumph.

Okay, now reread that last sentence. Do you see the problem with me raising the note overhead?

Here's what you should be asking: *How did Alley pull the note from his pocket if he already shoved it in the cubby?*

And here's what I should be answering: *The one I pulled out is the goofy version I wrote, not the serious version Rex wrote.*

Don't believe me? Read it for yourself:

Attention Cafeteria Staff:

Good news. After a reassessment of our budgetary concerns, I am pleased to direct you to reinstate the supplementary nutrition program—i.e., the free breakfast cart—immediately.

Sincerely,
Olivia Kugelmeyer

Wait.

Wait one second.

Now wait a *second* second.

That's not *my* note. That's the real note. Which means the one I tucked into the cubby is . . .

The hallway reels around me. "No! No, no, no!"

"Oh, Alley," Rex says, and puts a steadying paw on my arm.

"That means . . . ," I start, before gulping a few times.

"The note *you* wrote is in the mailbox," he finishes. "Which, if memory serves, is signed 'Principal Origami Kooglemire.'"

"They're going to know it's me," I whisper.

"That strikes me as highly probable."

"I'm so dead."

"The situation is, I'll admit, not an entirely cheerful one."

"Principal Kugelmeyer asked me to *not*!" I tell him. "This is not not. This is the opposite of not. This *is*."

Rex says, "Perhaps we might discuss strategies for recovering from this unfortunate octopus bananapants."

Or something. I don't know. I don't hear him, because I am rocketing back toward the office.

I need to grab that note before anyone sees

it—and this time there's no team. There's just me. Well, and Ms. D and Mr. D, and the principal, and the mail cubbies.

And the Boot of Fate, about to crush me underfoot.

20

Luckily, I remember the plan.

After galloping to the front office, I crouch at the plant, grab the pot, and stand. Except I *don't* stand. It's too heavy. Instead of standing, I squirt off behind the counter like a watermelon seed.

Still, I stick to the plan. As I flail behind the counter, I hurl popcorn kernels—

And I miss the coffee mugs.

The kernels pelt the walls and file cabinets. *Tunk, tunk! Tong, tung! Tat-tat-ta-rat-a-tat-tat!* It sounds like a steamroller driving across Bubble Wrap.

But I don't give up. I never give up! I keep trying, like Bubbie said. Without even glancing at the secretaries, I sprint for the cubbies, grab the awful note, and am almost totally home free when an urgent voice says, "Alllley!"

I pause, remaining calm, cool, and collected. What I am is unflustered. I have zero flust.

"What are you doing?" Principal Kugelmeyer asks from the doorway to her office.

I crumple the note in my hand. "W-would you believe 'nothing'?"

"Popcorn kernels landed on my desk."

"That part was an accident," I say.

She expands in her doorway like an inflatable principal. She looks, if I'm honest, not completely happy.

"What part *wasn't* an accident?" she demands.

"The, uh, running-into-the-office part."

"Which you did . . . why, exactly?"

I take a few breaths. "For the breakfast cart."

"How on earth, Alley, will kicking over a plant and throwing popcorn help with the breakfast cart?"

There she has me. That is what's known as "a good question." I almost congratulate her on the goodness of the question, but something in her expression stops me.

Instead, I say, "Buh."

Then, to drive the point home, I say it four more times. I'm about to make it five when another voice speaks.

This voice does not say "buh."

This voice says, "I believe Alley was attempting to convey an unpunctual fundraiser entry into the mailbox."

And with a faint crunch of carrots, Rex appears.

"You're trying to enter the fundraiser?" Principal Kugelmeyer asks me, deflating to her normal size.

"Gah," I say, which you have to admit is better than "buh."

"You want to join the bake sale?" she says. "To raise funds for the breakfast cart?"

"Precisely so," Rex says.

"Exactly thus," I say, backing him up.

"I'm pleased to hear that," Principal Kugelmeyer tells me. "But the fundraiser is tomorrow."

"The day after today," I agree politely.

"And the deadline for signup was yesterday."

"The day *before* today," I say, filling in the gaps.

She sighs and laughs at the same time. "Don't get your hopes up, Alley. One booth can't raise enough money to restart the cart. Still, why don't you show me your entry?"

"My entry?"

"The one in your hand."

"Oh!" I look at my note. "You mean in *this* hand? Yes, that makes sense. That is the entry you mean. The one—"

"If I may?" Rex says, and plucks the crumpled paper from my trembling fingers.

Then he hops over to Principal Kugelmeyer, pausing only to smooth the page on the table beside his briefcase.

And what he does next is, he hands her the note.

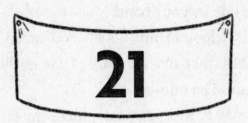

21

I'm sure that one day, when I'm a grizzled old man of thirty-six or forty-one, with a gray beard and skin like last week's cantaloupe, I'll look back at this moment and laugh.

Ha ha, Old Me will say. *Remember when Rex went completely haywire? What a funny moment that was.*

Then I'll go back to refurbishing earthworms or extending warrantees or whatever my job is in the distant future.

But right now, there is nothing funny about the *crinkle-crinkle* of Principal Kugelmeyer looking at a note.

There is nothing funny about the hum of

her laser eyes coming online, or the holographic crosshairs appearing on my forehead.

There is nothing funny about the USS *Alleykatz* preparing to divert all power to evasive maneuvers . . . too late, as hostile torpedoes lock on to my hull.

The enemy commander reads the note aloud:

To the Raisers of Fund,

This is me, signing up absolootly on time to help out with the bake sale! You must've missed this note when I handed it in last week.

Sixth-gradedly,
Alley Katz

Now, I am 90 percent sure that I can't do magic. I've reached into dozens of hats without finding a single rabbit. Every dollar I've torn in half has stayed in pieces. And if you pick a card, any card, the only thing that happens is you win a free card.

My one success was turning an ordinary beverage into an angry mob.

So how on all the earths did a perfectly reasonable note from me about the bake sale appear in the principal's hand? I definitely gave Rex the Origami-based note. And, I mean, I've never written a perfectly reasonable note in my life!

It's a riddle, scribbled on a jigsaw puzzle, hidden in a Maze of Mysteries.

So what I do is, I stare and blink. Not at the same time, of course. That's impossible. First I blink; then I stare. Blink, stare, blink, stare . . .

"You really want to join the bake sale?" Principal Kugelmeyer asks me.

"Like it says in my note," I tell her. "'Absolootly.' Which I wrote in my note, which is why I called it my note, because that's what 'my' means."

She eyes me. "You're not fooling anyone, Alley."

And just like that, I manage to stare and blink at the same time.

"We all know that you handed this in just now," she continues. "Not last week. Still, I suppose we can make an exception. What will you bring?"

"Bring?" I ask.

"To the bake sale, Alley. Brownies? Cupcakes?"

"Bagels," Rex murmurs.

The memory of sugared garlic-celery makes my eyes water. "B-bagels?" I stammer.

"Indeed," Rex says. "Your heinous homemade bagels."

The principal smiles at him. "I think you mean 'famous,' Rex."

"My mistake," Rex says.

"Great," I manage to choke out. "Good. Bagels! Coming right up."

"Why don't you study your history handout here in the office?" Principal Kugelmeyer tells me. "Instead of going to detention. Then you can leave early to start baking."

That's the word she uses: "baking."

Not: "smooshing in celery salt."

Still, this is great news. This is the superhero origin story of *Plan F for Fundraise!* My scrawny plan H just got bitten by a radioactive letterhead and transformed into a bulletproof scheme: sell enough bagel-doughnuts to pay for the breakfast cart.

I mean, I don't *want* to craft more bagel-doughnuts—I wish I could just wave a wand and fix everything—but sadly magic isn't real. Well, except for that note appearing out of thin air.

I guess *Rex* is magic. Think about it: he took the fake note from me, smoothed it on the table, then gave a totally different note to the principal.

Welp, some things are beyond human under-standing.

I just wish I could help Rex with his gym clothes problem. I feel bad about that, but he told me to focus on the breakfast cart. And Bubbie said I need to keep trying until I succeed.

So that's what I'm going to do. My other plans failed, A through R. The cart is still closed, and the kids are still hungry—and not hanging around the courtyard, chatting and chewing like I used to.

But not for long. I'm going to fix this. I'll *make* Plan Fundraise succeed.

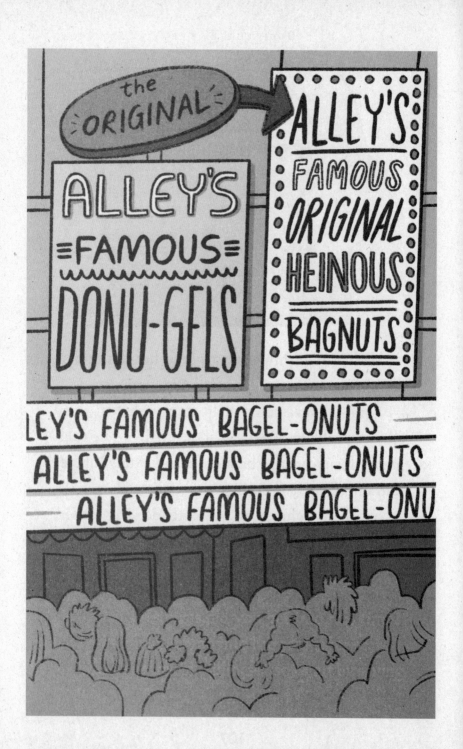

22

But first I need to read my history handout. And I speed through . . . until I hit paragraph three.

I told you the Silk Road isn't made of silk, right? Well, now I learn it's NOT EVEN A ROAD. It's a *bunch* of roads, and even some boat rides.

More lies! Still, at least there were caravans with spices, weapons, jade, and tentacled wool: everything you need for a fantasy game.

The name still bugs me, though. Things should be what they're called. Like, if a gym teacher says, *You must wear a* silk *uniform*, you can't wear a jade or spice uniform instead. Not even if you called them silk.

Maybe on Earth 14, "silk" doesn't mean silk

and "uniform" doesn't mean uniform. But on Earth 1, words mean what they mean!

What if they didn't?

That's what I'm asking myself when I'm hit by the biggest brainstorm of them all.

This isn't just a brain*storm*—it's a brainado.

I'm about to start paragraph four of the handout when I realize that I'm not at school anymore. The brainado chucked me all the way across town to Bubbie and Zayde's place.

I'm in the main room, collecting doughnuts. Some stale, some fresh. Some chocolate frosted, some glazed, some with sprinkles.

Bubbie raids her friends' apartments for hot pepper flakes, dill weed, and a bag of poppy seeds. She also brings me a dozen flaky cinnamon rugelach: "Just in case you get hungry, *bubeleh*."

Which doesn't make sense, considering I'm neck-deep in doughnuts. Still, I wolf down three rugelach to be polite, then reach for the celery salt. That's my signature flavor.

And finally I turn into a one-Alley bagel factory. Look closely.

I slice; I dip; I press.

I flip; I dip; I press.

I'm making three kinds of bagel-doughnuts. Spicy, with a layer of hot pepper flakes; dilly, with a crust of dill weed; and mild, with a dusting of everything.

Now *this* is a job for the twenty-first century. It's way better than earthworm refurbishing.

There are only thirty-one doughnuts, so spicing them doesn't take long. The next step is harder: I need to price them, which involves math, which is not my strongest subject.

Bubbie's even worse than I am. "Numbers shmumbers," she says. "They're all the same."

"I'm pretty sure they're not."

"So what're you learning in math class?"

"The order of operations," I tell her.

"I can tell you the order of *my* operations," she says. "First came my knee replacements, then the left hip . . ."

Luckily, Mrs. Green used to be an accountant. She helps us divide the amount needed to reopen the breakfast cart by thirty-one bagels, which comes to $129.03 per bagel.

That's way too much for even the dilliest of doughnuts. So I fix the pricing, then help with the sewing.

And pretty soon, I'm ready.

23

I don't always listen to Grannie Blatt, because she likes talking about clipping fingernails and cooking tongue in apricot sauce.

(Not her own tongue. A cow's tongue. I am not kidding.)

Still, I like what she said about tzedakah.

And Bubbie mostly agrees. "Justice is better than charity," she tells me. "But doing something is better than doing nothing, even if you're grumpy about it. Still, you shouldn't show off."

That's why I'm keeping my brainado quiet. I mean, *some* people will know. Not Rex, though. This is a secret from him.

So when I get to school early the next morning, the first thing I do is check that he's not around. Then I stagger into the courtyard with the breakfast cart . . . except it's still the courtyard *without* the breakfast cart.

Little kids, faint from hunger, litter the walkways and benches. Big, pleading eyes watch me. Stomachs rumble like distant thunder.

I dump the last of my Halloween candy onto a table, and the kids twitch like zombies who've scented brains.

"Alley Katzapult!" Mouse bellows, tossing an imaginary football to me. "Did you bring any jelly beans?"

I catch the ball and dodge imaginary defenders before spiking it at her feet. "No, but there's gummy bears. Those're in the same family."

Her laugh shatters a few windows. "Like bagels and doughnuts!"

I scan the area for cottontails. When I don't see any, I tell Mouse, "I need your help."

"With what?" she bellows.

"With my Secret Code," I whisper. "So don't bellow about it."

"I never bellow," she bellows.

I peer around one last time, then tell her, "All the sporty kids look up to you, right?"

"Most of them look *down* to me!" she bellows, then laughs like a fire alarm with a megaphone. "Because I'm short!"

"And there's loads of younger kids on your teams, right? Like, for example, fourth graders?"

"Sure!"

"So, if you start a trend," I say, "they'll follow along."

She makes a face. "No way, Alley! I'm not making little kids buy your dumb bagels! I can't believe you even asked!"

"I can't believe that either," I say. "Because I didn't."

"Not yet," Mouse bellows.

"Not ever!" I say. "My Secret Code is something else. . . ."

• • • •

I still need to keep Rex from learning my secret, so I watch him like several hawks.

The first thing I notice is that he's heading for the gym, which is strange for three reasons:

1) He doesn't have gym class now.
2) He's not allowed in gym class when he does have it, unless he wears the right clothes.

There are only two reasons, which is super strange, because I said "three reasons" a few sentences ago.

"Hey, Rex!" I call. "What's up?"

He turns at the gym doors and pats his briefcase. "I believe I've arrived at a strategy or scheme by which we might raise funds for the breakfast cart."

"You mean you have a plan?"

"Indeed."

"Well, I don't need it! I already have a plan. Even better, I have a secret plan." I'm not supposed to tell him about that one, though. "I mean foolproof. A foolproof plan. Plan F. So we don't need your strategy or scheme."

He eyes me like a bunny who does not believe any of his ears. "You have a plan?"

"F," I say.

"For Foolproof?"

"For Fundraise. But Foolproof works too."

"Are you certain?"

"You bet. *F* works either way."

"I mean, are you certain that you don't want to hear my suggestion?"

The truth is, I don't want Rex hanging around with me right now, because I'm afraid he'll guess my Secret Code. But did you hear that tone in his voice? He doesn't think I can plan!

So I snap, "Yes, I'm certain. I've never been certainer."

"Even so, if I might—"

"Shhh!" I say.

"—tell you my—"

"Double-shhh!"

"Truly, Alley, I think—"

"Stop thinking. I have already thunk!"

He sighs and says, "Very well."

Then he opens the door. And for some mysterious reason, instead of being filled with squeaks and shouts, the gym is filled with tables. And the tables are piled with containers. And the containers are packed with sweets.

"The bake sale!" I say, solving the mystery.

"Indeed." Rex clears his throat. "Are you positive that I may not share my plan?"

"As positive as a plus sign."

"Then perhaps I might ensure that your table adequately displays your goods?"

"Uh," I say. "You want to decorate the table?"

He pats his briefcase again. "Precisely. I happen to have art supplies with me."

"Yes! Good, thanks. You stay here and do that. Here." Because here is where he won't run into Mouse, who might accidentally bellow about the Secret Code. "In the gym."

"I shall," he says. "Now, will you tell me your plan?"

"I'll do better than that," I say. "I'll *show* you!"

And I pull the bagel-doughnuts—the bagnuts—from my backpack.

"You . . . cut them in half," he notes.

"Double the bagnut," I say, "at half the price. You do the math!"

24

Rex twitches a whisker at the sign with the prices. "You're charging $64.52 for half of a sugary doughnut that you encrusted with savory seasonings?"

"I rounded up," I explain.

"I'm afraid you've lost me."

"This is plan F, Rex. This is how I'll raise the fund!"

"Er," he says.

"At first," I explain, "I thought I needed to charge $129.03 per. But that's too high for a chocolate-garlic-celery-glazed bagnut, so I cut 'em in half and lowered the price."

Rex is so impressed he can barely speak. "How—I'm afraid—I'm unsure . . ."

"The other booths are raising money for art and music and stuff. So the breakfast cart is all us."

"Ah," he says.

"I told you it's a good plan!"

"It certainly is a plan." Rex wrinkles his nose. "And, er, you absolutely refuse to entertain my somewhat dissimilar approach?"

"No! Or yes. Whichever means I don't want to hear a word."

"If you are adamant, I suppose—"

"As adamant as Wolverine's elbows."

"Erm," he says.

"Don't worry, I've got this whole thing sewn—" I stop in a panic. That's almost a clue to the Secret Code! "Um, er . . ."

"Sewn up?" he suggests.

"No! What? Ha ha!" If I keep talking, I'll blurt the truth, so I say, "Well, I should be elsewhere. Elsewhere calls. Table away!"

As I turn to flee, he asks, "Do you happen to know where I might find Maya or Mouse?"

"No and no," I say, which is 100 percent true.

I mean, I know where they *are*. That much

I know. But I don't know where he'll find them. Because that depends on many things, such as if I tell him where to look, which I don't.

I know what you're thinking again, and this time I'm thinking the same thing: Why does he *want* to find them? Does he already suspect the Secret Code?

There's only one way to find out: by spying on him. And sure enough, during Quiet Study, I hear the gentle bellow of "Rexcalibur!" from the multipurpose room.

I slink closer and spot the Briefcased Bunny chatting with Mouse and Maya. This is a disaster! And I'm about to burst through the door to interrupt when I decide, for strategic reasons, not to.

• • • •

At lunch, I corner Maya and Mouse in . . . well, in a corner. That's the best place for cornering.

"I saw you in the multipurpose room," I say.

"Because we were there!" Mouse bellows.

"Aha! You admit it!"

Maya swipes at her phone. "The Mug contest is coming up."

"What were you two doing in there?" I ask.

"Loads of things!" Mouse bellows. "It's a *multi-purpose* room."

"And this time," Maya says, "I'm going to win that crown."

"According to my sources," I tell them, "you were talking with Rex."

"No we weren't!" Mouse bellows.

"Sure we were," Maya says.

I glare. "About my Secret Code."

"I don't even know what that is," Maya says.

"Oh, talking to *Rex*?" Mouse bellows. "Oh, sure, sure, sure, sure, sure. We were talking to Rex. Um, about Maya's game. Nothing else. No other secret with Rex! Just the game. On her phone! You know the one."

"*Realm Ruler*," I say.

"That's what we were talking about!" Mouse bellows. "With Rex! Rulers of the Realms! Nothing else. No *other* sneaky plan. Why would you think that?"

"Okay, cool," I tell her. "And you're still doing the thing I asked?"

"Sure am!" Mouse bellows. "And Chowder's helping!"

"Even cooler," I say. Chowder's basically a heart emoji that came to life, but he's in the sixth grade, so fourth graders will listen to him.

"How are you going to sell all those dough-nuts?" Maya asks, tapping at her phone.

"They're called bagnuts," I tell her. "*Bagel* dough*nut*. And how I'm going to sell them is out."

"Huh?" Mouse bellows.

"I'm going to sell out. Of them. I'm going to sell them all! I don't have a choice. I need to sell every last bagnut—"

"Or doughngel!" Mouse bellows. "For *dough-*nut ba*gel*!"

"—to pay for the cart." I sigh. "At least, that's plan F. I just hope it works."

"It'll work!" Mouse bellows.

"For sure," Maya says, swiping at her screen.

"Way better than you could possibly imagine!" Mouse bellows at me.

Which is pretty sweet of her to say.

25

My table at the bake sale is glorious. The big sign says BAG-NUTS? DOUGHN-GELS? YOU DECIDE!

The smaller signs say SPICY, DILLY, and MILD, and Rex chose a green tablecloth and drew pictures of wooden bagnut barrels. Which doesn't make sense—bagnuts don't come in barrels—but still looks cool.

And there's already a crowd! Though they're mostly grown-ups telling me I can't charge $64.52.

For example, one of the fathers says, "You can't charge $64.52."

See?

"What *are* these?" a mother asks, after sniffing a spicy bagnut.

"They're one of a kind," I tell her. "Unique items. You can't get them anywhere else."

That's my trick. Sure, they taste like the mutant offspring of barnacles and toothpaste, but everyone loves unique items. And admit it: You're a little curious, aren't you? You're wondering, just how bad *are* they?

You're not alone. Everyone is curious . . . but nobody is buying. The bake sale is two hours long, and after one hour I've sold a grand total of nothing.

"Plan F for Failure," Chowder says, plopping down beside me.

"Did Rex tell you to say that?" I ask.

"No." He frowns at a bagnut. "Do you have a plan G?"

I shake my head. "I don't even know what G stands for."

"Yeah, I don't either." His eyes brighten. "Oh, unless G stands for Graceful!"

"Huh?"

He gazes across the gym at Mouse. "Glamorous, generous, gumdrop—"

"Whoa, whoa—stop!"

"Gymnastic, gallant, gold-medal girl—"

"I have a plan," I yelp, trying to shut him up. "I have a plan!"

"You do?"

And, suddenly, I do. "Plan P. Do you know Mr. Morris, where my Bubbie lives?"

"Does he go to school here?"

"He's a hundred years old! He told me that when he was a kid, there were 'pullers' outside the stores. They'd shout at people, telling them to buy the stuff inside."

Chowder pales. "Please tell me you're not going to start shouting."

"I'm not going to start shouting," I tell him, because he said "please."

Then I stand in front of the booth and shout: "Get your bagnuts here! Best bagnuts in Earths One through Seven! Hot from the oven! Except . . . room temperature! Room temperature from the gym!"

I shout for twenty minutes and pull plenty of people to my booth. But none of them plunk down $64.52.

So I shout for another twenty minutes, and there is still no plunking.

Sure, everyone laughs and jokes and takes pictures, but I keep seeing the faces of those cart kids. I keep thinking about the juice boxes and cereal, the tangerine tosses and granola bars that the new crop of little graders won't ever enjoy.

It's wrong. It's unfair. It's unjust.

26

Working at my bake sale booth isn't the highest form of tzedakah, because everyone knows *exactly* who is shouting and pulling. I have twenty minutes to sell sixty-two bagnuts . . . and I don't know how. I promised those kids I'd bring the breakfast cart back, but what if I can't?

Then Rex rabbits to the booth, and I feel even worse. Why didn't I listen to his plan? What if he says, using ten-letter words, *I told you so*?

The worst thing is, he'd be right. "So" is exactly what he told me.

"The entire school," Rex says, "is talking about your booth."

"Which is looking good!" Maya says, filming me on her phone.

"However," Rex continues, "the bake sale is scheduled to conclude in fifteen minutes."

I hang my head. "Yeah."

"You tried," Chowder tells me.

"Ah, Charles," Rex says, "Isabella mentioned that you look slightly stiff."

I don't know what he's talking about. Charles? Isabella? These are just sounds. Then I realize he is talking about Chowder and Mouse.

Chowder's face lights up, and he starts doing his swaying dance. "Isabella thinks I look stiff!"

"Now you look like a toy soldier melting in a microwave," I tell him.

"I'm stretching!" he says. "This is what sporty kids do. We stretch."

"What might occur," Rex asks me, for absolutely no reason, "if your baked goods were subjected to an abrupt drenching?"

"You mean if the bagnuts got wet?" I ask.

He nods.

"Like with water?"

He nods.

"Like right now?"

He nods.

"Then this whole thing would be a complete catastrophe," I tell him.

"In that case," Rex says, "you might consider taking immediate action to avert—"

That's where I stop listening. And not because "immediate action" is my all-time favorite type of action.

Because Mouse throws a water balloon at me.

Not just any water balloon, one of my dodgeball water balloons. The ones I'm trained to catch.

I leap like a gazelle and catch the balloon.

I'm about to yell at Mouse to stop when she throws another one.

Now, I didn't tell you my Secret Code, because it's a secret. You don't need to know. Some things will remain a mystery. But I'll tell you this: the Secret Code is not THROW WATER BALLOONS AT ALLEY.

Not even close.

Why Mouse thinks this is the

plan, I do not know. And I can't even correct her, for two reasons.

One, Rex is right there. I don't want him knowing the secret.

And two, I'm busy catching water balloons.

I snatch at the second balloon—then Mouse hurls a third, and a fourth!

She throws them in a wild pattern of high and low, left and right, and I don't have a second to think.

I jump; I spin; I catch!

I toss the balloons aside.

I jump; I crouch; I catch!

I toss the balloons aside.

I skip, hop, dive, and catch again. For a moment, I forget the bake sale and the breakfast cart. I forget Maya filming, Chowder stretching, and sheep tentacling.

I am one with the dodge. There is no ball—well, *balloon*—that I cannot catch.

Until the unthinkable happens.

You'll never guess. That's what "unthinkable" means.

Here, I'll prove it to you. Take this quiz:

DOES ALLEY . . .

Miss a balloon?
Miss two balloons?
None of the above.
Some of the above.

Wrong!

I don't miss a single balloon.

What happens is, Mouse runs out of balloons. I caught them all, and there isn't a single drop of water on my table!

This is a sign. My luck has changed. My bagnuts will start selling by the dozen.

I'm about to do a victory dance when I realize that the gym is completely hushed. Nobody's talking; nobody's walking. Everyone is just standing, staring.

Not at my triumph. Not at my absolute victory.

What they're staring at is the balloons I gently tossed aside.

A thousand urgent voices cry, "Alllley!"

27

I give up.

I know I said that I never give up, but I'm done.

I didn't sell a single bagnut; I didn't save the breakfast cart.

I let those kids down.

I don't know why Mouse threw water balloons. I don't know why Maya stood there filming or why Rex didn't help. All I know is that I failed.

And that I spent an hour cleaning the gym, before slouching home.

My parents ask how my day was, but I just grunt and close my bedroom door. I flop onto my bed and try not to cry.

I don't want to talk about it—so I won't.

Instead, here's a picture of happier times on Earth 29.

28

Let's skip to the next morning.

I wake up early to bring snacks to the courtyard for the last time. There's nothing left in the kitchen but tea bags and tofu, so that's what I bring. Maybe someone likes cold, raw tofu. You never know. There are people who like *tongue*.

When I trudge into the courtyard, I'm staring at my sneakers. That's why I don't see it at first.

I don't know what Absolute Hero filled the cart with goodies. I don't know what Magnificent Legend wheeled the cart into the courtyard.

But I *do* know they're standing right behind me, because everyone turns to look. A thousand big eyes stare and—for some reason—tinny video game music plays.

The yard monitor says, "Allley!" which is bad.

Principal Kugelmeyer says, "Alllley!" which is badder.

Then she grabs my arm, which is baddest.

"I asked you to *not*," she tells me.

"Yeah," I say, ducking my head.

"But you didn't not."

"Sorry."

"Instead, you raised enough money to bring back the cart."

I unduck my head. "I muh?"

"You went about this completely backward, Alley. You should know better. Still, you worked so hard and you cared so much. I'm proud of you."

"Buh?" I say.

"First you made those horrible doughnuts and charged a ridiculous amount, to attract attention."

"Well," I tell her. "Um."

"Then you and Chowder started dancing."

"Oh," I tell her. "Erm."

"And that video." She chuckles. "But next time, think of a plan that doesn't involve water balloons."

I stand there for a while, reeling in shock. Just reeling and reeling. But once I'm fully reeled, I hear what the principal said: *that video.*

Sure enough, there's a video playing on the School News TV screen that faces the courtyard. And Maya is there with her phone, playing the tinny video game music.

Then a voice you might recognize bellows, "Alley Katztastrophe!" and cart kids start chanting "Al-ley, Al-ley, Al-ley," waving banana peels like flags, toasting me with juice boxes.

Treating me, in short, like an Absolute Legend and Magnificent Hero.

And I watch the video.

That's me, in front of my booth—which is the same green as the *Realm Ruler* tavern, with barrels that match the game barrels!

In the video, Chowder is writhing like a dizzy elf, and I'm doing a full-on Ogre Disco. I reach high; I bend low. I spin, I snatch, I reach . . .

"Wh-when?" I stammer. "Who? Why?"

"That's you," Maya says. "Yesterday. Raising funds by the truckload."

"But I didn't sell anything!"

"I posted the video to the Goblin's Mug."

"Of me *dancing*?"

"Yeah. The *Realm Ruler* gamers saw you raising money for school by selling the grossest doughnuts ever. For a totally stupid amount of money. They loved that. Everyone loved that. It's so weird!"

"It's just math," I mutter.

"Then you started dancing."

"But I didn't!"

She watches the TV screen. "Look at you go! Every move is perfect."

"I don't even know that dance," I say.

"You're doing the dance of the goblin king," she tells me. "But *I* won the crown. I won the Monthly Mug!"

That's when I realize what I'm doing on the video: I'm catching water balloons.

Mouse threw the balloons in that weird

pattern to get me to dance like the goblin king! To make me crouch and lunge and spin in exactly the right way.

This whole thing was planned to the inch by some sort of absolute mastermind.

"Plan A for Alley," Maya says. "That's what Rex called it."

I gape at her. "This was *Rex's* plan?"

"Yeah," Maya says. "Pure genius."

"Pure evil," I say, but I can't help smiling.

"Hundreds of gamers donated through the school website, and look!" Maya points to the full cart and the happy kids. "We did it!"

And you know what? I guess we did.

29

I find Rex just before his gym class.

"Hey, devil-bunny!" I call, jogging to catch up with him. "Are those ears or horns?"

His glasses flash. "I presume you watched the video?"

"Yes, you cottontailed genius!" I give him a twirling hug. "You single-pawedly raised enough money for the cart."

"I disagree. It was emphatically a group effort. You, Maya, Chowder, and Mouse all played parts. Yours, I might add, was of foremost importance."

"Why didn't you just *tell* me to dance?"

"You forbade me to address the matter."

"You mean I wouldn't let you talk?"

"Precisely so."

"Well, I only did that because"—I almost say something about the Secret Code—"that's what I did."

"Indeed," he says. "So. Today is Friday."

"Day after Thursday," I say.

His ears droop. "And this particular Friday, I must wear the physical education uniform or accept official punishment."

"But you're not wearing it," I say.

"Indeed," he says, and looks so sad that I almost tell him the truth.

Instead, I say, "Well, I've already got detention, so at least you won't be alone."

"That is a comfort," he says.

He doesn't look comforted, though. He looks sad. Still, he squares his shoulders bravely and continues toward the gym doors.

Then he opens them and stops.

Rex peers upon a warren of fellow bunnies— and a smile spreads across his face.

Which makes me smile too, though I try to look confused.

"What *is* this?" he asks, so surprised that he uses short words.

"Looks like a dress code to me," I say.

Like a Secret *Dress Code,* I don't say. I also don't say, *If a Silk Road can be made of boat rides, then a gym uniform can be made of bunny ears. And if every kid in fourth grade PE wears bunny ears, then bunny ears are the uniform.*

"Alley!" Rex says, his ears sproinging happily. "Are you claiming that you are not responsible for this turn of events?"

"Are you claiming that *you're* not?" I ask, quick as a flash.

He blinks. "I am perfectly aware that I'm not."

"I'm also perfectly aware of that!" I tell him.

"That is hardly—"

"Get in there, young bunny," I say, nudging him forward. "There are balls to be dodged."

He takes one step before stopping. "Thank you, Alley."

"Don't thank me," I say. "Just remember what I told you."

"What's that?"

"You," I say, "were born to hop."